CONTENTS

An artist's view of life along the Nile

SCHOLASTIC HISTORY READERS™

LEVEL
3
AGES 7 AND 8

EGYPT

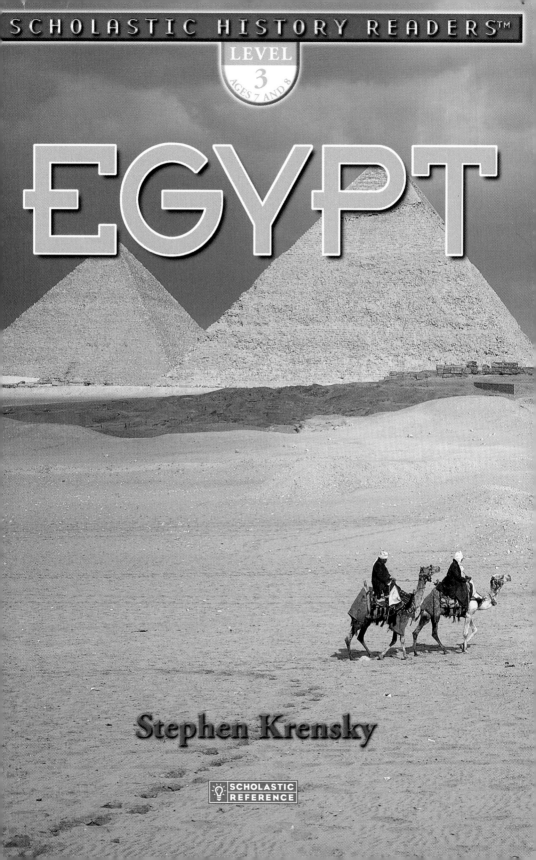

Stephen Krensky

SCHOLASTIC REFERENCE

PHOTO CREDITS:

COVER: SuperStock. Page 1: SuperStock; 3: Musee Du Louvre, Paris/SuperStock; 4, 7: North Wind Pictures; 8: Valley of the Kings, Thebes/Kurt Scholz/SuperStock; 9: By courtesy of the Board of Trustees of the Victoria & Albert Museum, London/Bridgeman Art Library, London/SuperStock; 11, 12: The Granger Collection, New York; 13: Christie's Images/SuperStock; 14: James McMahon/SODA; 16, 17: The Granger Collection; 18, 19: SuperStock; 20: Scala/Art Resource, NY; 21: SuperStock; 22: Newberry Library, Chicago/SuperStock; 23: British Museum, London/ET Archive, London/SuperStock; 24: Maynard Williams/SuperStock; 26: North Wind Pictures; 27: SuperStock; 28: Musee Du Louvre, Paris/SuperStock; 29: British Museum, London/Bridgeman Art Library, London/SuperStock; 30,31: SuperStock; 32: Archeological Museum, Florence, Italy/ET Archive, London/SuperStock;34: Egyptian Museum, Cairo, Egypt/Giraudon, Paris/SuperStock; 35: North Wind Pictures; 36: Erich Lessing/Art Resource; 37: Egyptian National Museum, Cairo, Egypt/Silvio Fiore/SuperStock; 39: Erich Lessing/Art Resource; 40, 41, 42: SuperStock; 43: Erich Lessing/Art Resource; 44: SuperStock.

Library of Congress Cataloging-in-Publication Data available.

ISBN 0-439-27195-9

Book design by Kristina Albertson and Nancy Sabato
Photo Research by Sarah Longacre

10 9 8 7 6   05

Printed in the U.S.A.   23

First trade printing, September 2002

We are grateful to Francie Alexander, reading specialist,
and to Adele Brodkin, Ph.D., developmental psychologist,
for their contributions to the development of this series.

Our thanks also to our history consultant, James F. Romano, Ph.D., curator, Department
of Egyptian, Classical, and Ancient Middle Eastern Art, the Brooklyn Museum of Art.

CHAPTER ONE

THE RIVER

The people living along the Nile River 7,000 years ago did not know much about it. They did not know that the Nile flowed from faraway mountains or that it ran for more than 4,000 miles (6,400 kilometers). They had no idea it is the longest river in the world.

They did know that the Nile was their only source of water in northeast Africa. They also had discovered that each summer its banks overflowed for several miles (kilometers) on both sides. When the water fell back, it left a dark, muddy **silt** behind. This **kemet**, the Black Land, was perfect for farming, and became the name of their country.

As people learned to raise crops in this rich soil, their settlements grew.

This artwork shows men drawing water from the Nile.

The wall of an Egyptian tomb pictures a harvesting scene.

By 4500 B.C., several large villages had developed in Egypt. They were supported by two crops a year. The first harvest was wheat and barley, the second was vegetables like beans and peas.

The river also provided the people with other sources of food, including fish and ducks.

This painting shows a group of people gathered on the banks of the Nile.

These early Egyptians worked together, digging ditches and canals to channel the annual floodwaters. These irrigation projects both kept the flooding under control and increased the size and richness of their farmland. These projects also gave the Egyptians experience measuring and marking things carefully.

They also charted the passing days to create the first calendar based on the sun. Their year of 365.25 days was amazingly accurate. It had twelve months of thirty days each and five extra days to mark the birthdays of their gods. This calendar helped them predict when floods would come along the Nile.

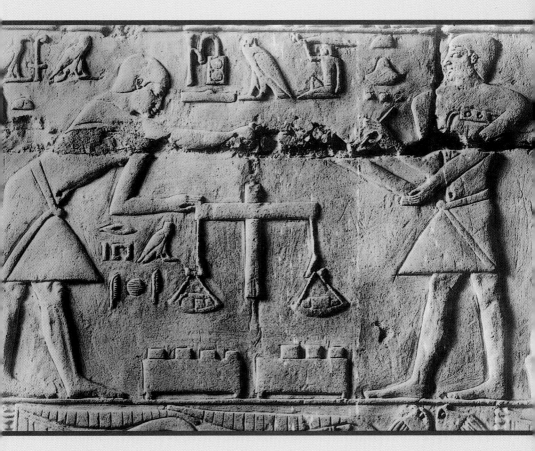

Artwork decorating a tomb portrays one man weighing gold while another man records the weights.

This man's crown indicates that he was a king of Lower Egypt.

In the next few hundred years, two major kingdoms developed by the Nile. One was to the south, in Upper Egypt. The other was to the north, in Lower Egypt.

Each kingdom was centered on the narrow bands of useful land bordering the Nile; the river was always a strong link between the two kingdoms.

EGYPTIAN GODS
The Egyptians had hundreds of gods including **Ra (Rah)**, the sun god, and Osiris, the king of the underworld. They believed that the underworld was the place souls went to after death. The Egyptians believed that the Nile flowed from a pot held by the god **Hapy (Haap-y)**.

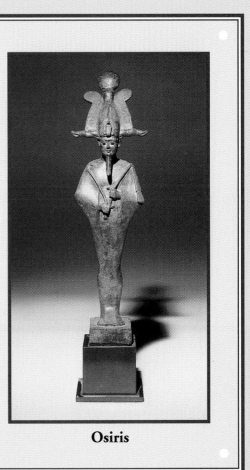

Osiris

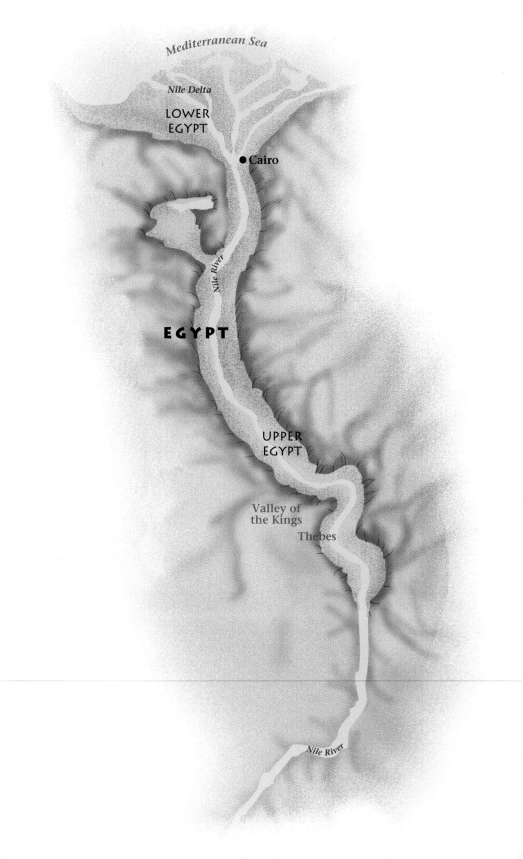

CHAPTER TWO

RULING AND WRITING

When the kingdom of Upper Egypt grew strong enough, it expanded its control into Lower Egypt. This new, single Egyptian empire was created around 3100 B.C.

Though the king, later called a **pharaoh** (**fair**-oh), was its supreme ruler, his power was still based on laws. He could act harshly when necessary, but he was also respected for showing mercy and kindness.

A temple gateway shows a carving of a pharaoh.

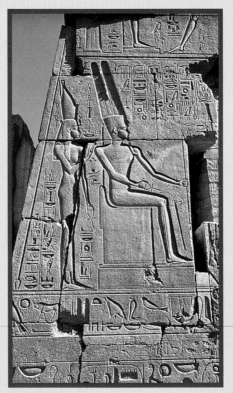

Statues of pharaohs line the walls of this temple court.

The kingship in Egypt was usually passed down from father to son. Rulers that came from the same family were part of the same **dynasty** (**dye**-nuh-stee). When there was no child to inherit the throne, a new dynasty would start when a powerful **noble** or general seized the throne.

This is a gold mask of the boy king, Tutankhamun.

Some of the Egyptian kings were more famous than others. One was the great builder Khufu (**Khoo**-foo) (2551–2528 B.C.). Another was the boy king, Tutankhamun (Tut-ank-a-**moon**) (1333–1323 B.C.), whose tomb was opened thousands of years after he died, with all of its riches still inside.

A third was the most powerful woman pharaoh, Hatshepsut (Haat-**shep**-soot) (1473–1458 B.C.), who ruled alongside her nephew before declaring herself king.

Queen Hatshepsut sometimes wore a false beard for official ceremonies.

Of course, every king hoped to be famous, so they all wanted a history kept of their reigns. At the same time, increases in trade brought a greater need for record keeping.

Carvings on this stone list bread, beer, cattle, incense, and other items.

*Special carvings called cartouches
were used for royal names.*

To fill these demands, the Egyptians
invented a kind of picture writing called
hieroglyphs (hye-ur-uh-**glifs**). It used
simple drawings of people or animals or
flowers to represent either ideas or sounds.
Egyptians used hundreds and hundreds of
these picture symbols.

Hieroglyphs could tell a story, explain laws, or order a shipment of grain. The writing itself was often painted on walls or carved into soft stone. Sometimes it was written on papyrus (puh-**pye**-ruhss), a thin paper-like material made from the stem of the papyrus plant.

A fragment of papyrus includes both a partial drawing (left) *and hieroglyphs.*

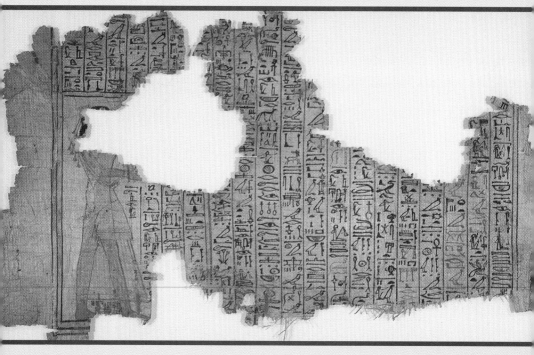

THE ROSETTA STONE

People stopped using hieroglyphs more than 2,000 years ago. The understanding of these symbols disappeared. The symbols remained a mystery until modern times, when the Rosetta Stone was studied in the early 1800s. The stone itself was found accidentally by some French soldiers in 1799 near Rosetta, Egypt. Dating from 196 B.C., it displayed an ancient decree in three scripts, including Egyptian hieroglyphs and Ancient Greek. Language experts who knew Greek were then able to translate the hieroglyphs.

Most people, though, never learned to read or write these hieroglyphs. Specially trained scribes did almost all of this work themselves. And as Egypt grew in power, the scribes were very busy keeping track of everything that happened.

King Tutankhamun and his queen are shown beneath the rays of a golden sun.

CHAPTER THREE

DAY TO DAY

During the long centuries of Egyptian rule, both kings and peasants lived according to the same principles. Once Egyptians found a way to do something, they stuck with it. They didn't try to improve things or make progress for its own sake.

For example, it might take 100 men to move around a heavy stone building block. Since 100 workers were always available to do this, no one ever tried to figure out an easier way to move the stone.

Men at work erecting a temple are portrayed in this artwork.

Tomb art shows a queen playing a board game.

The Egyptians simply did not think life should be viewed as a struggle or a challenge. However, this did not mean that everyone lived the same way.

A father, a mother, and their children pose together in this ancient Egyptian sculpture.

Most Egyptians lived simply. Grandparents, parents, and children often shared one mud-brick house. The walls were plastered, and small windows were set high off the ground.

There was little furniture. Everyone sat on the floor, and they ate off mats rather than a table. Their meals were mostly meat, vegetables, bread, and beer, with fish or duck eggs to broaden the menu. Children had time to play and owned toys like balls, tops, and board games.

This Egyptian doll can be seen in the British Museum in London.

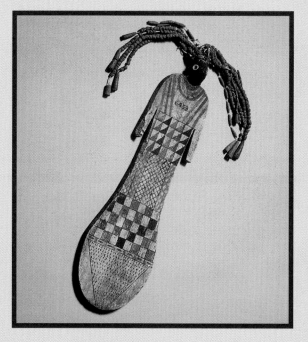

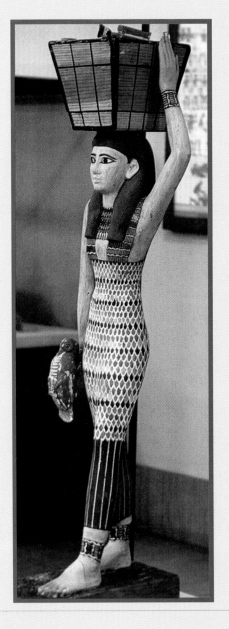

Wealthy nobles, however, spent their time in grand manors with many rooms and views of the river. They had servants to run their households and to see to their needs. Their clothes were woven of the finest linen, and their meals might include pigeon stew, honey cakes, and fine wines.

A young woman carries an offering of food to a tomb.

MAKING BREAD

Egyptians ate a lot of bread. It was made of flour that had been ground between stones. Some of the crumbled stone ended up mixed into the flour and then into the baked bread.

Examining the remains of ancient Egyptians has shown that many of them had poor teeth from chewing on grit over the years.

Rich or poor, there were no schools for the general population. Only the smartest children were given an education, in schools called Houses of Life. People such as farmers and bakers only learned enough to do their jobs, which changed little from one generation to the next.

An Egyptian tomb painting shows the preparation of a mummy.

CHAPTER FOUR

MUMMIES AND MONUMENTS

As much as the Egyptians enjoyed their lives, they were not afraid of death. They did not believe that death was an ending. When a person's **ka**, or soul, left this world, it moved on to another place.

But the ka did not go alone. It needed clothing, food, and other possessions to be comfortable in its new surroundings.

A cup like this, in the shape of a lotus flower, was found in King Tutankhamun's tomb.

*A drawing based on tomb art illustrates
a soul being weighed in judgment.*

The process started while the body
was prepared for burial. First, most of
the dead person's internal organs were
removed and put in jars. Only the heart
was left in the body. The Egyptians
believed the heart would later be weighed
by the gods to judge the worth of the
person who had died.

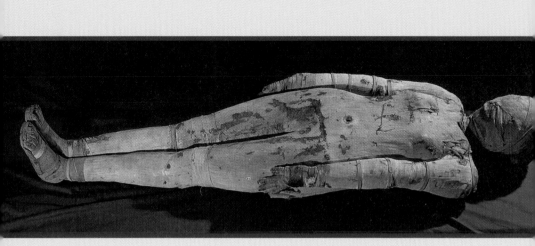

This is the mummy of a young woman.

The body was then soaked for many days in natron (**nay**-tron), a natural salt, before being treated with ointments and wrapped in linen bandages. Afterward, this **mummy** was placed in a decorated coffin.

It took over seventy days to mummify the body of a pharaoh or noble. The pharaohs also planned the most impressive burial sites. This tradition began with simple graves that included tools and household goods.

This richly decorated box belonged to King Tutankhamun. It was found in his tomb.

But around 3000 B.C., wealthy people began building larger tombs for themselves. These **mastabas** (**mah**-stah-bahs) had several underground chambers covered with a roof above the ground. The bigger the space, the more that could be put inside it.

The first pyramid, a royal house for the dead, was designed for the pharaoh Djoser (**Jo**-sir) (2630–2611 B.C.). It was built of stone and is 203 feet (62 meters) high with a base measuring 409 feet (125 meters) by 341 feet (104 meters). Every block was cut and placed with precision requiring great mathematical skill. Unless the stones were joined correctly, the pyramid would not stand securely.

The pyramid built for Djoser looked
like a huge staircase with six steps.

When most people think of pyramids, they think of triangular shapes like these.

Later pyramids adopted a triangular design with smooth sides. These pointed toward the sun and the sun god, Ra. (The Egyptians thought that the sun's rays would give the pharaohs strength as they climbed up to the gods.)

The largest was the Great Pyramid, built for the pharaoh Khufu. It is 478 feet (146 meters) tall and made of more than 2,000,000 stone blocks. It may have taken twenty years and tens of thousands of workers to build it.

Visitors from all around the world travel to see the Great Pyramid.

Khufu also built the Great Sphinx (**sfingks**), a giant sculpture with a human head on a lion's body. The Sphinx is 69 feet (21 meters) tall and 243 feet (74 meters) long, and it stands guard over the pyramids nearby.

The Great Sphinx attracts thousands of tourists each year.

THE VALLEY OF THE KINGS

In addition to the pyramids, magnificent tombs were also built into desert cliffs. The most famous ones are found in the Valley of the Kings at western Thebes. Many of the later pharaohs were buried there.

Altogether, there are more than eighty pyramids still standing today. Most are in sight of the Nile River, which still flows to the sea as it did when these giant tombs were built.

The Nile River is still an important part of Egyptian life today.

The Nile River remains as important to Egyptians today as it was to their ancestors, who created a civilization that lasted for almost 3,000 years.

CHRONOLOGY

4500 B.C.	Early settlers come to the Nile Valley
3100 B.C.	Hieroglyphs are developed; Early dynasties begin
2630 B.C.	First stone pyramids built for Djoser
1674–1547 B.C.	Egypt conquered and ruled by Hyksos from Syria-Palestine
1539–1080 B.C.	The New Kingdom, Egypt's wealthiest and strongest era
1473 B.C.	Hatshepsut, a woman, becomes pharaoh
1333–1323 B.C.	Reign of Tutankhamun
332 B.C.	Egypt conquered by Alexander the Great
196 B.C.	Rosetta Stone created
1799	Napoleon's soldiers discover the Rosetta Stone
1881	Mummies of 10 pharaohs discovered in one tomb
1922	Tutankhamun's tomb is discovered
1987	Tomb for 52 princes found in the Valley of the Kings

▲ ▲ ▲ GLOSSARY ▲ ▲ ▲

B.C.—A way of naming years in the distant past by measuring backward from one year in Roman times. (Our own years—like 2001, 2002—measure forward from that same year.)

dynasty (**dye**-nuh-stee)—A group of kings or queens who are related to one another in an unbroken historical line

hieroglyphs (hye-ur-uh-**glifs**)—A form of writing that uses picture symbols to show words and ideas

ka—The soul or spirit of a person, which moved on to another world after the person's body died

kemet—The wide strip of rich farmland on both sides of the Nile. Kemet was also the ancient name for Egypt.

mastabas (**mah**-stah-bahs)—Rectangular stone structures built over tombs

mummy—The specially prepared remains of a body buried in an Egyptian tomb

noble—A person ranked above common people (often related to the pharaoh)

pharaoh (**fair**-oh)—The king or leader of the people in ancient Egypt

silt—A rich sand-like dirt found at the bottom of rivers

INDEX

NOTE TO PARENTS

A whole world of discovery opens for children once they begin to read. Illustrated stories and chapter books are wonderful fun for children, but it is just as important to introduce your son or daughter to the world of nonfiction. The ability to read and comprehend factual material is essential for all children, both in school and throughout life.

History is full of fascinating people and places. Scholastic History Readers™ feature clear texts and wonderful photographs of real-life adventures from days gone by.

FOR FURTHER READING

ALIKI. *Mummies Made in Egypt.*
New York: Harper Trophy, 1985.

MANN, ELIZABETH. *The Great Pyramid.*
Illustrated by Laura Lo Turco.
New York: Mikaya Press, 1996.

MILTON, JOYCE. *Mummies.*
New York: Grosset & Dunlap, 1996.